#4

THE *SWOOP* LIST

FEEL REAL GOOD

STEPHANIE PERRY MOORE

darby creek

MINNEAPOLIS

Darby Creek
A division of Lerner Publishing Group, Inc.
241 First Avenue North
Minneapolis, MN 55401 USA

For reading levels and more information, look up this title at
www.lernerbooks.com.

Cover: © Hemera Technologies/AbleStock.com/Thinkstock (teen girl);
© Andrew Marginean/Dreamstime.com (brick hall background); © Andrew
Scherbackov/Shutterstock.com (notebook paper).

Interior: © Andrew Marginean/Dreamstime.com (brick hall background);
© Sam74100/Dreamstime.com, pp. 1, 34, 70; © Luba V Nel/Dreamstime.
com, pp. 8, 41, 77; © iStockphoto.com/kate_sept2004, pp. 15, 49, 83;
© Hemera Technologies/AbleStock.com/Thinkstock, pp. 21, 56, 90;
© Rauluminate/iStock/Thinkstock, pp. 28, 63, 97.

Main body text set in Janson Text LT Std 12/17.5.
Typeface provided by Adobe Systems.

Library of Congress Cataloging-in-Publication Data

The Cataloging-in-Publication Data for *Feel Real Good* is on file at the Library
of Congress.
ISBN: 978-1-4677-5807-9 (LB)
ISBN: 978-1-4677-6052-2 (pbk.)
ISBN 978-1-4677-6194-9 (EB pdf)

Manufactured in the United States of America
1 – SB – 12/31/14

For
my gents

Jaylen Allen
Akil Baddoo
Julian Buffaloe
Saige Burgan
Tyler Edwards
Ar'Mon Hickson
Mark Jones
Justin Pouncil
Kristian Richard
Andrew Roberts
Brandon Thompson
Richard Walker

You are outstanding young men,
and I am so thankful to work with you.
Feel real good about your accomplishments!
You are dynamic!

CHAPTER ONE

Denying (Sanaa's Beginning)

For the swoop list girls, spring was in full bloom as the month of April was about to usher itself into their lives. Though their friendship was tighter and they were happy with graduation nearing, they still had drama. Coming together at the end of every month for a slumber party to vent, share, and connect had become a ritual for them.

This time, Sanaa Mathis was the only one unable to sleep. She just kept looking at old pictures in her phone of her and her boyfriend, Miles. Their topsy-turvy relationship seemed to have run its course. Sanaa ended the relationship when Miles wanted to take things further.

Letting him have his way with her used to be a plan she was down with, but since her name wound up at the top of the swoop list, she had decided she wanted to move on.

"Why you starin' at him like you wanna devour him or something?" her good friend Willow Dean asked, startling Sanaa. "Ain't y'all over? He probably ain't losing no sleep over you."

"Why you always up in my business? I thought we were over you talking to me any kind of way?" Sanaa questioned.

"No, I told you that I'm a little brash."

"Yeah, and you also said you'd work on it because you know I don't like it."

"What don't you like? The way I'm saying it, or what I'm saying? Because I'm being really honest with you, Sanaa. You're practically drooling over a guy you ended things with."

Sanaa wiped her mouth. She knew deep down inside that she really did miss Miles. She didn't understand why there was such a big tug-of-war going on in her brain and in her heart, and it upset Sanaa that Willow could clearly see she wasn't done with this guy.

"Just stay out of my freaking business," Sanaa said as her voice rose. "Everybody doesn't need to always hear exactly what you're thinking. Can't you make people feel good instead of always making them feel bad?"

Working her neck, Willow shouted, "If the truth makes people feel bad, then they need to do a check in the mirror!"

"What are y'all yelling about?" Olive Bell woke up and asked.

"For real," said Pia Alvarez, who had also woken up. She went over to Sanaa and asked, "What's wrong?"

Sanaa yelled, "I'm just sick of her always trying to analyze people and put them down! She thinks she knows me, but she doesn't!"

"I don't know you!" Willow hollered from across the room. "I don't know that your tail is two-faced—you screwed your best friend over for the man you promised you'd get for her." Willow was talking about Sanaa's former best friend, Toni. And she wasn't done.

Willow went on, "And that you are bipolar—giving it up one minute, and now all of a

3

sudden you wanna act like a virgin. Yet, now you pining after the guy's picture, like you wanna jump him. I do know you . . . be clear in that!"

"Oh my gosh, Willow!" Octavia Streeter said. "Chill!"

"Whatever. I don't even care," Sanaa lied.

"Of course you care," Pia told her. "Or else you wouldn't be so rough under the collar and upset about all of this."

"We're supposed to be encouraging each other to feel better when we hang out. Not being so tumultuous that we don't wanna be around each other," Olive said sternly. Then, she added, teasing Willow, "Do I need to go and get your mama?"

"My mom is an advocate for speaking the truth," Willow said back to Olive.

"Yeah, but she's a preacher. She can pray over us," Olive said. "I believe the devil is real, and I'm not gonna let him come against our friendship. Now what?" When Olive said that, both Willow and Sanaa went into their respective corners and settled down.

"Good, I'm glad y'all are quiet! This is freaking me out. Look!" Octavia said as she held out her cell phone for the other four girls to see.

Dear Swoop List Girl,

Life can be mighty challenging when you're on the list. First you're ostracized by your peers, and then you personally feel horrible because you've been placed on the list in the first place. I know for me, the pain and stigma that it caused in my life were unbearable. But, I hope you and your friends have paid heed to my first three notes. You've stopped doing what you were doing; you've started to believe in yourselves; and you've let past mistakes make you stronger. If you've followed my other advice, now is the time to give back.

If we're all honest with each other, we all want to feel real good. Feeling good can come from a touch, from a great grade, or from feeling pretty. I challenge you to work together to think of ways that you can feel really good by giving back. So many girls in middle school, and elementary, and high school, believe it or not, need to hear your story. Share it. Make the world a better place. If you've learned anything from being on the swoop list that can help somebody else, pass it on before you pass like me.

Your Angel, Leah

"That's just creepy. Just so creepy!" Octavia said.

Pia responded, "I know, but maybe that is just what we need to do. Help others."

"I'm down with that," Willow said.

Olive started shaking and said, "Yeah, because we certainly don't need to be fighting. I guess everybody needs to check her phone. I'm tryna see if that Leah girl wrote me another letter. But look what just posted instead."

Olive held her phone out, and Sanaa read a post from Toni: "We're tired of Sanaa and her stank crew talking smack. Now it's time to smack them down. Me and my new girls are ready to bust up the swoop tricks."

Sanaa backed away. "Is she crazy?"

"Is she trippin'?" Willow said, completely

having Sanaa's back. Willow was so hot you wouldn't have thought that she and Sanaa had any dispute earlier.

"Yeah, I mean, I don't understand why she would say we've been talking about them. Ain't nobody been talking about them," Olive uttered.

"They wish we were talkin' about them," Pia said. "Since we formed an alliance, everybody's been wanting some type of connection with the swoop list girls, positive or negative."

Octavia went over to Sanaa, put her hand on her back, and said, "Girl, it's alright. We got your back."

"I just can't believe this," Sanaa finally uttered.

Willow said, "Well, Sanaa, you need to believe it. You've been worrying about some . . . you know what? I ain't gon' belittle myself and say the name she deserves to be called. But I hope now you can see she means you no good. Quit worrying about her. She don't love you back. To that, there's no denying."

CHAPTER TWO

Regretting (Willow's Beginning)

Willow was so fed up with folks putting down the swoop list crew. Not since she'd socked Hillary from the dance team a month ago had she felt like she put someone in their place. Now she had a new mission. She'd been giving Sanaa a hard time about Toni, but Willow really didn't like Toni anyway. In Willow's eyes, Toni was snotty. Willow had caught her laughing at folks' clothes. Willow knew Toni was salty because she'd tried out for cheerleading every year but didn't make it. Toni's scores barely landed her on the dance team. Willow remembered seeing Toni and Hillary in the corner, rolling their eyes her way. Reflecting on that made her even hotter.

Willow shouted, "Y'all need to get your stuff. We're going on a ride."

"A ride? It's the wee hours of the morning," Pia uttered in a weary voice.

"Whatever! Let's roll," Willow said as she picked up Sanaa's keys.

Sanaa said, "I don't want to go and fight Toni or anything crazy like that."

"We're just going to scare her tail," Willow said. "Don't you be scared."

"I'm not scared. I'm just trying to squash all this," Sanaa boldly stated.

"But how can you squash all this when she's taking it to a whole other level?" Willow lightly popped Olive in the arm. "Come on, Olive, have my back."

Olive threw her hands in the air. "Nuh-uh, Willow. I will ride with you, but I'm with Sanaa on this one. I've seen where violence can lead, and I don't want no part in it."

"Y'all get in the car. She going to put all this stuff out on the Internet, trying to make people think we're punks? We'll show her tail. I'm not scared of her at all, and the swoop list girls shouldn't be either. She wants a fight . . . she going to get one."

About three minutes later, all five girls were crammed into Sanaa's car. Willow was behind the wheel. She wasn't driving recklessly, but she wasn't driving the speed limit either.

"Tell me where I'm going!" Willow demanded of Sanaa. "Where's that heffa live?"

"Why do we need to go by her house?" Sanaa said as she looked at the other girls, hoping they would help her persuade Willow to turn back around.

"Don't be looking over there at them," Willow blurted out in anger.

"Y'all, we're just going to drive by. Without us even having to do or say anything, we can put our hearts and minds together to come up with something that will change Toni's mind from acting a fool."

Willow didn't care that the other girls just looked at her. They didn't want to go by at all, but if this was the compromise, they had to take it. Clearly, Willow wasn't going to back down until she did something.

"Alright, fine. Turn right up here," Sanaa said.

"That's what I'm talking about. People are going to continue to poke at us until they understand that they can't do it. We got to make them not want to do it. We got to make them respect us," Willow declared.

"But don't you think the way Leah suggested doing it in her letter is better than us retaliating on people?" Octavia offered in a timid way.

"Don't be scared to tell Willow what you think. Speak up," Olive told Octavia. "Because I agree with you, Octavia. Willow, you need to stick to what you say. If we're just driving by there, fine, but sometimes you got to let people know you not studying them. You give people too much time of day, then they keep on messing with you. It can blow up in your face."

Sighing, Willow said, "I got y'all. Where do I go now, Sanaa?"

Sanaa sighed. "Turn right, then left. Her house will be on the right. Fifth one down."

"We better hope we get back before your mom notices we're gone," Pia said. "Last thing I need for her to do is alert my mom that I was misbehaving. We finally got some trust going on in our family."

Frowning, Willow said, "My mom is dead asleep. She and my dad are all curled up. Tired probably from getting busy like they used to do when they were in college."

"Uh, TMI!" Pia squealed.

"Really!" Sanaa said. "I mean, that's good and all, but we don't want to know their business like that."

Willow laughed. "Don't get me wrong. I'm happy they are working through whatever, but they are a little too loud for my and my brother's taste sometimes. They so old, but they wear each other out so bad that a bomb could go off and they wouldn't wake. You know what I'm saying?"

Tired of hearing her, Sanaa said, "Okay, girl, that house right there."

Willow abruptly turned the car to head into the driveway that Sanaa pointed out. "Well, you could have told me! I was about to pass it. You ain't want to tell me. That's wassup."

Willow turned off the car and told the girls to get out. None of them wanted to get out. Finally, she got out by herself and walked up the driveway.

Willow felt she needed to have everyone's back, so she started screaming at the house. "You want to try and front the swoop list girls! We're here! Come on out, Toni! You want to put something all on the Internet like you all big and bad? We right here. Come and do it! Come and get it! I know you scared."

Though Toni lived on an isolated street, her house was not the only one on it. Lights started popping on. The car horn went off as Willow's friends tried calling her back. But Willow stayed big and bold. When Toni's front door opened, Willow was spotted.

"Young lady, get off of my property." A male adult stared at Sanaa's car. "What, Sanaa? Is that you?"

Suddenly, Willow spotted the adult coming toward her. She turned and ran. She got back into the car.

"Oh my gosh, he thinks you're me, huh? Toni's dad thinks you're me? Oh my gosh, Willow! How could you do that?" Sanaa expressed.

All the girls grilled Willow, but she didn't care, not until they got back to her place. Not only was Willow's mom up and completely reprimanding them all for leaving the place, but Olive found a video that someone from Toni's house must have posted, showing Willow ranting and raving and going crazy in the driveway. The caption read, "What else can you expect from the lunatic swoop list girl?"

Watching the video, tears dropped from Willow's eyes, and she wondered why she couldn't get out of her own way and take the advice of her friends. Most of the times when she did things her way, she was the one who ended up regretting.

CHAPTER THREE

Frustrating (Olive's Beginning)

The next morning, Olive was actually happy to go back to the group home. Though she enjoyed being with the swoop list girls and was happy they were able to rally around Willow to get her to understand that she needed to chill some with her antics, there was no place like home. Although Olive didn't have two parents, she still felt loved at the group home. And what made it even more special was the fact that Charles, her boyfriend, was on his way back to it after being temporarily banned by a judge because of his reckless behavior. If she had her way about it, Charles would already be there when she arrived.

As Sanaa dropped her off, she saw Olive's eyes beaming with pride. "Your boo is back, girl."

Sanaa nudged Olive in the arm. Both of them watched as Shawn and Charles moved Charles's boxes back inside. Olive was eager, but timid.

"Go on and get out, girl. He's looking over here and not at me," Sanaa teased Olive.

Olive saw something in Charles's eyes that was different. She didn't want to admit she was apprehensive about reconnecting. While he was gone, she had texted him, called him, and e-mailed him, all to no avail. He hadn't responded.

Intuitive, Sanaa said, "Don't even worry about a thing. Act like everything's alright. He'll get in line where you lead him."

"You sure about that?" Olive asked, looking at her friend.

"Yup, I am. I know Miles would kill for me to speak to him, but right about now I'm not giving him the satisfaction."

"That's the difference," Olive explained. "I'm more like Miles, wanting to reconcile and get everything straight. But Charles is like you. I think he's done with me."

"Well, if Charles is like me, let me give you a little hint. I'm not done with Miles. He's too deep in my blood, but I'm not gonna let him control me. And if Charles is thinking you're trying to control him, explain to him why you're not."

Olive reached over and hugged Sanaa. She got out of the car and found the confidence to walk up to Charles. "Can I help bring something in?"

"Yeah," Shawn said, still unable to pick up the big boxes himself. He was recovering from the injury he'd endured when he got shot by Olive's ex-boyfriend, Tiger, and his guys during a drive-by. The police hadn't proved that it was Tiger and his gang. However, Tiger bragged in school and elsewhere that he did it. Tiger also bragged he had cops on his payroll. Olive knew Charles was still furious he wasn't able to retaliate, and she knew he was still furious at her, too, when she saw his standoffish way.

"Naw, I don't need your help," Charles

abruptly uttered as he grabbed the box from Olive's grasp.

"I don't mind. I can take a couple boxes in. They are not that heavy. Let me help."

"I'm sick of your help. Like I wanna be movin' back in here anyway. I didn't need your help with the judge, okay? You stuck your nose in where it didn't need to be. Now I am forced to come back here. And check this out, like my new jewelry?" Charles said in a mean way as he lifted up his pants leg and showed her the ankle bracelet he had to wear for the judge. "I'm on house arrest. You happy, Olive? House arrest."

"Alright, man. Back up, dang. You know she ain't want all this," Shawn said.

Charles vented, "You right. I should be mad at both of y'all."

"Me?" Shawn uttered quickly, trying to get himself out of harm's way.

Charles responded, "Yeah, you. I'm sure you were around here moping, making her feel bad that I was gone. And then she did something stupid . . . begging and pleading with the judge to send me back here, and now I'm back. I told you I didn't need your meddling. I don't know why you couldn't have just left well enough alone."

Olive felt the tears starting to well up, but she refused to let them fall. If it's one thing she'd learned from the swoop list and one thing she learned from Tiger, she had strength. And though much had been taken from her—her virginity, her dignity, and even her sanity—she was trying to regain some normalcy in her life. Letting a man get the best of her was no longer in the plan.

"Fine!" she yelled out.

"Fine!" Charles screamed back.

"Okay, you two actin' like kids," Shawn said. "Both of y'all know your tail's happy the judge reversed his decision. And Charles, I don't care what you say, man. You about to graduate. You droppin' out of school because you want to take a job? Shoot, please. You better live off the state a little while longer. I can't go nowhere anyway for fear my gut might pop back open with these stitches that ain't quite healed. So, it ain't like you gotta be around here alone, and Olive ain't got no car to be drivin'. We both can keep you entertained while you on lock."

Charles threw down the box and said, "I don't need her to stay here."

Olive put her hand toward his face and screamed, "I didn't ask to stay around you! I just wanted you to have another chance. I just wanted to fix what I'd messed up. And contrary to whatever you believe, I didn't need Shawn to make me feel worse than I already did. And, I don't need *you* to make me feel any worse than I already do. I'm sorry I screwed stuff up so much. I'm sorry things aren't perfect, but I'm not sorry that you're back. And if you don't ever speak to me again, it'll hurt, but I'll be alright. Because in a minute, I'm going to somebody's college, with or without your trifling, ungrateful behind. Be an idiot, because trying to talk any sense into you is so frustrating."

CHAPTER FOUR
Bonding (Octavia's Beginning)

Octavia didn't know how to feel. On one hand, she was excited that her dad and Shawn were bonding. But on the other hand, the two of them were bonding so much she was getting squeezed out.

"So y'all are going fishing?" Octavia asked when Shawn, unbeknownst to her, showed up at her door.

Shawn smiled. "Yeah, I'm excited."

Frowning, Octavia said, "But you two fished last week. And yesterday you were with him, playing on his work's baseball team."

"What? It's a problem if I hang out with your

dad? He said he'd pick me up after work, but Ms. B said it was fine if she brought me over," Shawn explained. Ms. B was the foster mother at the group home where Shawn lived with Charles and Olive. "So, I thought it was cool if I made it easy for him and came over here. I thought you'd be happy to see me for a minute."

"I just get to see you for a minute, and you think that's okay with me?"

"So you upset or something?"

Of all the things to be mad at a potential boyfriend for, Shawn getting closer to her dad wasn't one of the things Octavia wanted to put on that list. It wasn't like he was cheating, angry, or avoiding her. She just hated to admit to herself that she was jealous of her own father.

"Come here," Shawn said as he put his arm around her shoulder. "You know you're beautiful, right?"

"You don't have to say that," Octavia said to him, feeling truly self-conscious.

"Wait, why do you resist when I pay you a compliment? I see your face in my dreams. I just want to put my fingers all through that sexy, fiery-red hair of yours," Shawn uttered as his hands did just what he said.

Octavia stepped back. "Sexy? Fiery? Those words are so opposite of me, Shawn. And maybe that's why my dad is able to take all your attention. Yup, if I had some of those qualities, I could keep your attention better."

"Don't be coy. I never had a male figure who wanted to spend time with me. I'm not trying to take your dad away or anything."

"No, no, no. I know he's always wanted a son. And I mean, he's been a great dad for me, but tea parties and dolls truly wasn't his thing."

"I'm not trying to play little race cars with him either, Octavia," Shawn said.

Octavia could tell by his body language that he was getting upset. He shook his head, folded his arms, and turned away. She felt he wasn't too happy feeling belittled. She nudged him gently.

"Ease up. I understand what you're saying. I would never tell Ms. Davis this because I wouldn't want to scare her, but she's been more of a mom to me than my own mom." Ms. Davis was the school counselor who had been a lot of help to Octavia and the other swoop list girls. "I'm glad that my dad can be there for you. So don't get me wrong on that."

"I guess I'm a little confused as to what you want from me. You say you understand. You say you want attention. But when I give you attention, you think it's contrived, or you think you don't deserve it. I don't know. I guess I don't know what else to do."

"Hey! There's my partner," Octavia's father said as he opened up the front door with much cheer. "You haven't been waiting on me too long, right? I don't want to leave you two guys alone in my house."

"No, sir. I just got here," Shawn said as he stood up to shake her father's hand.

Her father said, "Naw, I know you're good. I trust you with my girl. Just give me one sec. I'm going to change clothes, and we'll be out of here."

"No problem, sir, take your time," Shawn said respectfully.

Before Octavia and Shawn could resume talking, her father called out from his bedroom.

"Octavia, sweetie! Come here for a sec."

"Yes, sir."

Normally it would take her five seconds to walk to her dad's door, but she was taking her time. She pondered over what to tell him. A part of her wanted to express the fact that she wasn't pleased with the two of them connecting. But she knew that would be too selfish, so she sucked up her pride and went into the bedroom.

Her father said, "Come in, hun. You alright with this, right?"

She was so puzzled by the question. Had she not done enough to hide her true feelings? Did he just know her that well? If she answered truthfully, would he back off? And if he did back off, would Shawn forgive her? She rationalized in her mind and decided that not rocking the boat was the best option.

After a moment of hesitation, Octavia uttered, "Yeah, Dad. It's fine."

"Okay, because I know we've been spending a lot of time together, but you've never taken interest to a young man before. I'm excited that this guy is really cool. Of all these jokers around the city of Jackson, you've picked a real good one."

At that point Octavia was irritated, feeling her father liked Shawn because he pretty much liked everything her father liked. However, she was really surprised when he said, "He's a good one because he likes you. Can't stop saying cool things about my Octavia."

She couldn't help but smile after hearing that. She felt she needed to quit tripping, let go, and let the guys have fun without her feeling some type of way.

Leaning over and kissing her brow, her father said, "Well, you and I are going to hang out soon."

"Okay, Dad, but Shawn is really grateful that he is able to connect with you."

"Right. But I know y'all are young, and I know you guys want to have some time. I'll be out in a minute. I'm sure you can keep him company until then," her father said as he winked.

Octavia quickly went out to Shawn. She pulled him close and gave him a big kiss. Neither of them were pulling away.

Finally, Shawn jerked back and said, "I know your dad is coming, so I don't want to get caught touching his baby girl. But I hope it was good."

"Oh, it was," she said, melting in his arms.

"Thank you for sharing your dad with me. I want him to like me because I want him to think I'm good enough for you. I think he approves because of this quality time he and I have spent bonding."

CHAPTER FIVE
Changing (Pia's Beginning)

Much in Pia's life was a little different from the way it used to be. Her mom was acting more responsible. She had close girlfriends who expected her to share everything. Her high school years were soon coming to an end. More importantly, the police felt they had enough evidence to make an arrest in her rape case. She couldn't feel too confident because it always seemed to be something. However, she wanted desperately to relax and enjoy the new direction her life was going. So she took a deep breath, smiled, and entered Jackson High School.

"Where my girls at?" Pia said out loud. "It's going to be a great day."

"It's not going to be too great of a day," Kenny, a basketball player, said as he grabbed her arm and yanked her behind a row of lockers.

"Ouch! Let me go!" Pia grunted.

Another basketball player, Isaiah, grabbed her mouth, squeezed it tight, and started cussing at her. She started shaking. Her mind raced back to the night of the terrible ordeal, and she became petrified.

"You listen here," Kenny said. "We tried to talk some sense into Stephen, thinking he saw what he saw, but he won't listen to reason. You could ruin us. We trying to graduate ... just like you. You don't know it was us, do you?"

Pia knew that she had heard these guys talking in February before basketball practice. She knew that these were two of the voices of the three guys who had bragged about having their way with her. And one of them had even been so bold to say he wanted to rape her again.

If Pia's hands were free, she would have slapped them both. She realized her legs were free, so she got herself together and kneed Isaiah in the groin.

"Ow!" Isaiah buckled. "You take back what you said about us! You stop making false accusations. You know you enjoyed it just as much as we did!"

Pia and Kenny looked at the guy she'd kneed. Isaiah had just admitted that they were the ones who were with her that night. Kenny got Isaiah up from his crouched position and jammed his buddy up against the lockers.

Kenny attacked, "How could you let her know that it was us? How could you say it was us? What are you? Stupid!"

Pia moved to get away. Unfortunately, she wasn't quick enough. Kenny yanked her long hair, put his hand on her face, and smashed her head back against the locker.

"You forget what he said. You don't want this to keep going on. You don't want to end our lives," Kenny told her.

Fed up, Pia spit in his face. "Urgh, you ended the life of my baby! That's right! I got pregnant that night! The two of you and your other friend took advantage of me!"

"So you're pregnant?" Isaiah asked.

"No . . . I'm not pregnant anymore. How could I have a monster's baby? But you aren't the only ones who've got to worry about your life being different. My life will never be the same. I ended a pregnancy, and it haunts me every day. I can't even sleep some nights, thinking about how y'all forced my legs apart and laughed while each of you forced yourselves on me! Not even bold enough to show me your faces! I cheer for you at basketball games, for goodness sake! I was in your corner. I've heard your voices, and now Isaiah admitted it. You all even bragged about it in school! And yes, Stephen is bold enough to stand up when he didn't before. He saw y'all. You are not getting off!"

Kenny was about to punch her when someone yelled, "What are y'all doing?"

Pia turned to see Ms. Davis coming to her rescue. Before the two boys could run off, Ms. Davis told Pia, "You go on to class. These two are going to the office."

Isaiah whimpered, "But Ms. Davis, we were just . . ."

"Save it!" she said to them.

As Pia went on to class, she wiped the tears that had fallen. She didn't mean to become so emotional, but how could she hold it together after coming face-to-face with two of her three attackers? They were kids, just like her, with bright futures ahead. She couldn't make it easy for them. No way. She wasn't trying to feel better about putting them away, but she realized maybe justice would make her feel whole again.

Pia wasn't looking where she was going, and she stepped on something. It was like a tree limb that broke in half. When she looked down, she saw the broken stem of a red rose. When she bent down to pick it up, she saw more roses all lined up on the floor, leading toward the cafeteria. She heard a lot of commotion that way. She was hungry and could have used a biscuit, but she didn't want to be around people. She'd just walk by fast and get to class.

But as soon as she rounded the corner, she saw a group of people standing around some guy who was holding a bundle of roses in his hands. And when the crowd moved away, she could see Stephen's face. He was pointing with the roses to a poster with the letters *P-R-O-M* and a question mark on it.

Prom was the last thing Pia was thinking about at that moment. However, when she looked into Stephen's eyes, she could see he was so sincere. The tears she'd tried to stop earlier started falling again. She could hear the girls oohing and ahhing and the boys grunting. Dressing up like a princess was such a refreshing thought, particularly with this handsome guy who would not back down this time from saving her honor. So she nodded. Stephen picked her up and spun her around. She was so happy that her day and life had gone from bad to good. Her life was changing.

CHAPTER SIX

Fighting (Sanaa's Middle)

Everyone was all abuzz. Word had spread around school quickly about Sanaa's friend, Pia, being asked to the prom so romantically and publicly. The swoop list girls were texting each other.

"Let's meet up after school 2 celebrate!" Olive texted.

Willow texted back, "Yeah! One of our own made all the girls envious. Go Pia!"

"We need 2 meet up now," Octavia texted in. "It's important. Can't wait."

"K on the way," Sanaa texted back.

The bell had rung, and Sanaa knew where their spot was located. She just wondered what in the world could be wrong now. As she walked through the crowd of students, people started looking and pointing at her. She knew it wasn't good.

As soon as Sanaa saw Octavia she threw up her hands and said, "What is it?"

Panicking, Octavia grabbed Sanaa and squealed, "They want to fight us after school! Did you hear me, Sanaa? Your girl and her crew want to fight all of us."

Frustrated, Sanaa said, "What? I'm not fighting. We're about to graduate. Nobody is getting kicked out of school."

"Look!" Octavia showed Sanaa her phone.

There was a text from Toni. It read, "The swoop list girls better bring their butts to the park at four. They're going to show up to peoples' houses and try to punk them out late at night . . . we're going to end this once and for all and put the sluts in their place!"

Sanaa was livid. She was angry at Willow for giving these girls the ammunition to keep up the horrible feud. And she was even more pissed at Toni for being so mean and vindictive.

As Sanaa pondered what she was reading, Olive and Willow rounded the corner.

"Look, y'all! They want to fight us!" Octavia yelled out with idiotic excitement.

Sanaa thought she was crazy. Octavia seemed scared and yet happy about the pending brawl. Sanaa wanted her to chill.

"I say we take them down," Willow said. "We need to shut them up. They sent that text to a bunch of people. We can't have people thinking it's okay to mess with us."

Olive voiced, "Yeah, I'm getting sick and tired of people talking about us too. We've been through enough. We got to end this, and if knocking a heffa in the mouth is what's going to do it, then I'm ready."

"Violence is not going to settle nothing," Sanaa told them.

"Well, your butt is going," Willow declared, looking at Sanaa like she knew she better not leave her hanging.

"Tell her, Olive!" Willow said.

Olive nodded and added, "Yeah, Sanaa, this is your girl starting up a lot of this trouble. You got to be there. We're all in it now. Real talk, you got to lead the way."

Sanaa had no clue how she was going to get out of this, but they did have a point. She wasn't fooling herself. It was her ex-best friend pushing all of this. She couldn't leave her new girls hanging.

"Fine," Sanaa grunted. "After school. Meet me at my car."

"That's what I'm talking about!" Willow yelled. Willow snatched Octavia's phone and texted, "It's on. —SLG"

"What's SLG?" Octavia said.

Willow boldly said, "The swoop list girls! They'll figure it out! Calling people a punk. I'ma show their butts."

As soon as the girls walked away, Miles walked up to Sanaa with a box of six cupcakes in his hand.

"Hey," Miles said. "I know we haven't talked in a while, but . . ."

Rolling her eyes and scurrying, Sanaa said, "I'm trying to get to class."

"Well, just take this."

"I don't want any cupcakes."

"You want these."

As Sanaa looked closer, she noticed that on each cupcake was a toothpick with a little flag at the top with words he had written. When he saw her looking at the carton, he pointed to how he wanted her to read them. One cupcake said "prom." The next one said "will." Then another one said "you." Another one said "go." Another one said "with." And the last one said "me."

Sanaa just shook her head and walked on past him, leaving him with the box of cupcakes to do with as he pleased. Sanaa didn't think about him for the rest of the day.

The day flew by as the talk of the school moved from Pia being asked to prom to the swoop list girl fight.

After school, all five girls scrunched into Sanaa's car and she drove straight to the park. Last thing Sanaa wanted to do was fight, but she knew she was too far in to turn away. When they got there, a crowd was already forming. It was like people had skipped their last period class to get a front-row seat for some massacre that Sanaa really wanted no part of.

When Sanaa parked the car and got out, Pia got out of the back, walked up to her, and said, "Are we really supposed to fight?" Pia hadn't made it to their meeting in the hallway earlier that day. She'd been too busy fielding questions about her romantic prom proposal. It didn't surprise Sanaa to hear that Pia wasn't into fighting.

Pia went on, "I don't want to fight. Octavia may try to act like she wants to, but I know she does not want to either. It's Willow and Olive who think that they're gangsters."

"None of you girls are going to have to fight!" Sanaa yelled out before she turned to the crowd. "Where are you?"

The crowd parted. Toni stepped forward. Her new little crew was right behind her.

Sanaa stepped to Toni and said, "This is between me and you. My girls don't need to fight."

"Oh, this is more than just between us. All of y'all rolled up on my property late at night trying to take me by myself. Now that I got backup, you talking about it's between me and you . . . please!" Toni put her hands up like she was ready to fight.

Sanaa put her arms up in surrender. "You want to hit me? Hit me."

"What are you doing?" Willow said. "Ain't no need to give up. We're ready."

"I'm not letting you do this. Get back," Sanaa said as she turned back to her nemesis. "Toni, you're mad at me. You got something to say, or if you want to hit me . . . fine. I'm right here, right now. This is ending because me and my swoop list girls, we ain't punks. We ain't pushovers. But also be clear, we're not fighting."

CHAPTER SEVEN

Sharing (Willow's Middle)

"Let me just whoop up on this heffa!" Willow yelled out as she charged at Toni.

Sanaa caught her and held her back. "No, Willow, I'm serious. It's gonna be none of that."

"You can't punk out. We gotta represent," Willow tried to egg Sanaa on.

But Sanaa challenged her, "Remember the other night? You were sick to your stomach with regret. All these chumps out here got their cell phones out, ready to record us, post the drama, and make it ten times worse than it's actually gonna be. You know you my girl. We're bigger than this. You told me it's Toni's loss. I'm done trying to kiss up behind her. I showed up to show her exactly where I stand. If she wants to fight the air, then that'll be her looking stupid. But today, the swoop list girls are done with the pettiness." Sanaa turned around and walked away.

Pia, Octavia, and Olive followed. Willow was having a hard time just taking off. Even though Sanaa made a good point. It took one stank look from Hillary, the girl who had been on the dance team with Willow and who led the charge in making Willow quit the team, to make her uneasy.

Willow walked over to Hillary, pointed her finger in her face, and said, "Look, you know I can beat that tail. Be glad my girls told me to turn the other cheek, because I wanna bust you in your lip." And the way Willow said it, Hillary stepped back. "Right. I knew your punk behind wasn't gonna fight nobody. So, to all the onlookers, you came, and you saw her step back."

Feeling satisfied, Willow left feeling really good that she played the confrontation smart instead of stupid. Before she reached everyone, her cell phone started vibrating. She knew it was folks posting the truth. However, when she looked down at her device, she saw that she was in a group text from Ms. Davis.

The text read, "Did you guys forget? You said you were going to come with me to the middle school to speak to some at-risk girls. Where are you all?"

"Willow! Come on!" Olive yelled out. "We gotta go and see—"

Before she could finish, Willow hollered back, "Ms. D. Yeah, I know!"

It took them all of ten minutes to get across town to the middle school. The middle school got out later than the high school. However, since they were late, they weren't going to have much time in the session.

All five of the girls had forgotten that Ms. Davis had asked them to do her a favor. They were going to be part of a roundtable discussion, keeping it real with a bunch of seventh- and eighth-grade girls who'd been having relationship trouble or were caught breaking some of the rules at the school. The swoop list girls, including Willow, were all nervous about divulging their most private mistakes.

"I just feel real unworthy to be talking to some fast-tailed girls about not being fast, when I was superfast myself," Willow admitted.

"Just be open with them. I don't have to monitor you guys," Ms. Davis said. "You know what to say and what not to say."

"There's about fifty girls out there," Octavia said after peeking at the boisterous crowd.

"And they each wanna hear from you all," Ms. Davis reassured. "Their parents have signed a consent form. So you all can dig as deep as the session warrants."

"Why are we doing this again?" Willow said as she scratched her head, wanting desperately to leave.

Ms. Davis said, "I promise you, when you give back, you'll feel great."

Willow stayed negative and said, "I don't think I'm gonna feel great by telling a bunch of young girls my mistakes."

"Trust me. Try it," Ms. Davis said as she patted Willow on the shoulder.

Fifteen minutes into the conversation, things really started heating up when one of the middle school girls said, "This boy I know really wants me to go out with him. But I don't like him that way. He kissed me once even though I said no. What do I do? Is it my fault that he won't leave me alone?"

Pia responded, "That was actually my story. It's not okay for him to being kissing you, or doing anything else, if you say no. I was raped. And I know I can't blame myself for what my attackers did. Don't blame yourself. But you should talk to a school counselor about this. It's not okay for him to be harassing you when you've made it clear you don't want him."

"Wow, thanks," the young lady said.

Another girl stood up and said, "My girlfriend likes this guy, but he likes me. I like him too, and I don't know what to do."

Sanaa winked at the swoop list girls and said, "I can answer that one. Don't keep it a secret. If she's really your friend, you gotta find a way to be honest with her. Keeping it from her will only hurt you both worse."

Another middle school girl said, "This rough but popular guy likes me, but sometimes he scares me because he's a little too aggressive."

The swoop list girls looked at Olive. She nodded and shared, "That was my story. When a guy shows you who he is, believe him. The apologies will come. It might be a little shove one day, a push the next day, a slap the next time, and before you know it, he'll be controlling you. He might ask you to do things that seem crazy. And because you believe that he cares about you, you might do them. Before you get in that deep, run the other way or get some help. Trust and believe that."

A little shy girl said, "Well, no guys like me, and I want to do something to shake it all up. I want attention."

Octavia stood and said, "Trust me. Being young and innocent is not a bad thing. You don't want to bring unwanted attention to yourself and do crazy things that you'll regret. Take it slow. Enjoy this time. Be open for the right kind of friends who will come in all different packages. Look at us. We're the swoop list sisters. We were a bunch of misfit chicks at first. But who would've ever thunk it . . . we showed everyone we are worthy."

A brash girl stood firmly and said, "Well, none of you got my issue. I like boys. And jealous girls tryna ruin my rep. Why should I stop having the fun they envious they ain't havin'?"

Willow said, "Girl, I stood in your shoes. I was the one with the worst reputation. So if you think it's okay to just be free and loose and stuff, it's not. A bad reputation follows you so many places. You might smile in a crowd, thinking it's great to have that kind of notoriety, but at the end of the day, you'll be crying on your pillow, wishing you could take it back. I learned the hard way that no one will take you seriously. Honestly, I now respect myself too much to give up the goods so freely."

The girl nodded. Willow smiled. She felt good being truthful.

When she saw Ms. Davis giving a signal for them to wrap it up, Willow uttered, "You guys are awesome. Don't compromise yourself. We've been there, we know. We've been on the worst possible list anyone could ever put us on. We did survive it, but it wasn't easy or fun. We're here because we don't want you all to end up like us. Make better choices."

The girls stood up and gave them a standing ovation. The swoop list girls hugged each other. Willow was happy they came.

Ms. Davis took the stage with the counselor from the middle school and said, "I'm glad you all came. I know these girls are going to be stronger because you all were genuinely sharing."

CHAPTER EIGHT

Defending (Olive's Middle)

When Olive and the swoop list girls stepped into school the next day, they were getting mad respect. People were smiling at them, nodding at them, and giving them thumbs up. They'd taken the higher road, and that was well received. The rest of the girls were smiling, actually more proud of the fact that they had made a difference in the lives of young people the day before, too, but Olive couldn't be as happy as her friends because she was still brokenhearted that Charles was walking around the group home, keeping her out of his world.

Seeing her down, Octavia leaned in and said, "Shawn told me things were still tense for you at home."

That was an understatement. Olive did not respond to Octavia at all. Octavia put her arm around her girlfriend and squeezed tight.

"You know deep down he does care about you. Look at him over there with Shawn. They're both checking us out," Octavia stated.

"Don't try and defend him," Olive uttered, deeply wishing Octavia was right, but knowing that wasn't the case. "Charles has made it pretty clear I'm the last person he wants to be associated with."

All of a sudden, they heard a bunch of commotion, like a group of people running. A crowd of students was gathering to their left. Olive wondered what was up, but she wasn't trying to find out.

"What's going on over there?" Octavia asked, walking toward the noise.

"Somebody just probably wanting to get attention before the end of the school year," Olive replied, walking away from the madness.

One thing Olive had learned was when a crowd gathered, you didn't have to be in the middle of it to figure out what was going on. She had made a commitment to herself to stay on her game. Stay in her own lane. Stay focused on what she had going on and flee crowds. Unless she knew what was up in advance, it was probably trouble. Even if Octavia wasn't going with her, she kept moving far away from the crowd.

"Uh, Olive. You might want to turn around!" Octavia yelled out.

"I'll catch you guys at lunch," Olive said without looking back.

But the stomping got louder, and Octavia caught up to her and turned her around. "Look."

It was the thugs in Tiger's gang, each dressed in a white T-shirt with a letter spray-painted on the front. Six guys were in a single-file line: Ice, a mean guy Tiger relied on, and a bunch of others. Her skin was crawling as they walked towards her. She could not forget the bad history she shared with them all.

Olive saw the letter *P* on Ice's chest, and he moved to the side, doing the snake dance.

Another guy's shirt held the letter *R*, and he moved in the opposite direction. Then a guy with an *O* on his chest followed Ice, revealing a guy with an *M* who went in the other direction. Then there was a guy with a question mark on his shirt. The guy bent down, and Tiger jumped over him with a wine glass and a bottle.

"I know he ain't bring wine to school," Octavia said to Olive.

"No," Olive said. "He knows sparkling grape juice is my favorite drink."

When Tiger removed the towel from the label, that's what it said. Grinning, he walked her way. The five other guys started singing, snapping their hands back and forth like they were in a boy band. Tiger chimed in.

"Go with me to prom?" Tiger sang all out of key. "I can rock your world if you'd be my girl for the night. Olive, be my princess, let me hold you tight. If we go to prom, you will be the bomb and the envy of everyone. Say you'll go with me, and we'll have a lot of fun."

Tiger started swaying, grinding, rolling, and rocking, and all the chicks gathered around started shouting and screaming like he was a star. Olive's face turned pink. Tiger hadn't been a good boyfriend when they were dating at all. At one point, he'd asked her to sleep with some of his gang members as a favor. Now, she couldn't believe he had the audacity to use those same guys to help him ask her to prom. Even after she'd done what he wanted and got busy with practically all of them, he'd still dumped her. She was dumb then, but months later, she was dumb no more.

Olive looked straight in his eyes, took the glass with grape juice, splashed it in his face, and said, "Heck to the naw!"

Then Tiger showed himself. "What? You gonna try and 'barrass me in front of all my peeps? I'm tryna make you come up. Tryna do you a favor . . . and put you on my arm. You ain't got no money to buy no dress. Don't get it twisted. That chump Charles ain't got a penny to his pocket."

Before Olive could respond she sighed. "See . . ."

Still upset, Tiger yelled, "See what? You

splash drink all in my face, don't accept my invitation, and think I'ma be cool. I went all out thinking about this, and you think it's supposed to be okay?"

"Okay, whatever, Tiger!" Olive put her hand in his face and turned around and walked away.

Tiger yanked her arm really hard, turned her back towards him, and said, "You going to go with me!"

"She ain't got to do nothing!" Charles said as he knocked Tiger's hand out of the way. "She don't want to go with you, she don't have to."

"Have you manned up and asked her to go to the prom with yo' broke tail?" Tiger got back in Charles's face and asked.

"That ain't none of your business. Just be clear she don't want to go with you."

"Like I care about what you got to say," Tiger said as he shoved Charles really hard.

Charles was about to charge him back, but Olive stepped up to him. "No, please. You already hate me because I got you in the middle of the stuff with Tiger. You're on probation."

Charles looked deep into her eyes and

said, "I'm not mad at you because you got me involved in something with Tiger. And as hard as I try to stay away from you, when I see him put his hands on you, I'll do whatever it takes. Because when it comes to keeping you away from him . . . I'll always be defending."

CHAPTER NINE
Devastating (Octavia's Middle)

"Is he gonna ask me to the freaking prom or what, y'all?" Octavia said, throwing a hissy fit at the fast-food restaurant with her swoop list girls.

Pia leaned over and said, "I hope he asks you, because I need somebody to go with."

"Whatever." Octavia nudged her. "You're going with Stephen . . . Mr. Million Roses."

"Yeah, but Sanaa and Olive told me they ain't going, and Willow got her nose up in the air. She ain't tryna say yes if poor little Dawson gets up the nerve to ask her," Pia said. Dawson was Willow's neighbor and former boyfriend. Their relationship had hit the rocks recently.

"So, when Shawn asks you, I'll be excited. It can be me and you and our dates, hanging at the prom. Not a perfect world, because all of us won't be together, but it'll be fun . . . if I go, anyway. I'm thinking about canceling on Stephen."

"What are you talking about?" Octavia voiced, saying what all the others were thinking.

"I don't have anything to wear." Pia looked down. "It's not like my mom can afford a dress right now. She's just getting on her feet. The last thing I wanna do is worry her about getting me something. I don't know how to break it to Stephen that I can't afford to go to prom, but that's my dilemma. I still wanna go so bad, but . . ."

Sanaa chimed in, "But money is tight. I understand parent job issues."

"All that stuff can be worked out. Money shouldn't keep people from going to the prom," Willow shared. "And a man ain't gon' keep me from going. Sanaa? Be my date, girl?"

"We're seniors. You don't mind stags?" Sanaa asked.

"Naw. We'll step in there beautiful and

show 'em. Make all the boys in the place wish they'd asked us. Well, not Shawn and Stephen, of course," Willow joked. "But the rest of them guys in there will be on my booty."

"See, you ain't got no type of sense," Sanaa said as she gave Willow a big high five, actually agreeing with her.

Willow said, "Olive, you should go with us."

"Pia's not the only one who doesn't have a dress," Olive said.

"I told you, we'll get that all worked out," Willow reassured her. "The church has some group they work with in Atlanta that does something with dresses. I don't know."

"Well, tell us about it," Sanaa said. "Quit holding out!"

Playfully putting her hands up to tell Sanaa to back off, Willow replied, "I don't know all the details."

"See, you get people up to let them down. Don't be sayin' you can help work things out when you don't know what's up," Pia joked back.

"You are trippin'!" Willow said. "We'll figure out all the details. Calm down. It's obvious that you don't want to tell Shawn you can't go, so heads up. We all going to prom."

"Speak for yourself, Willow," Olive murmured. "It's not just about a dress for me. I don't wanna go with my girls. If I can't go with Charles, I don't wanna go. And as much as he tries to act like it wouldn't bother him if I went with you guys, I know it would. So count me out."

Shocked and a bit disappointed, Willow checked her friend. "So you gon' let a man keep you from doing what you wanna do?"

Olive pushed back. "No. I'm gonna let my heart keep me from doing what I don't wanna do without him. You don't have to understand, Willow. We can agree to disagree, but it is what it is."

Willow rolled her eyes, not agreeing. Olive rolled hers back, not caring.

Octavia looked at them both and said, "Y'all just finish the ice cream. Y'all are supposed to be worrying about my problems anyway. I mean, why won't Shawn ask me? What have I done wrong, Olive? Why does he want to sit around the house on prom night?"

"For one thing, you need to quit worrying about it," Willow said, truly irritated.

"I agree with her," Olive said. Now the two of them were on opposite sides of the issue, but that's what Octavia loved about the swoop list girls. They never stayed mad for long.

Octavia voiced, "Alright, alright. I hear y'all. I'm not gonna worry about it. I know he's gonna ask me any day."

Three days later, Octavia was walking around like she'd lost her little puppy. She was talking with Olive as they headed to class, trying to find any clues to why Shawn had been so distant, but Olive seemed standoffish too.

Octavia bulldozed, "Okay, so what's going on, and what don't I know? Why won't you talk to me? We're supposed to be girls, but you won't tell me what's up. Did I offend you? Did I offend Shawn? Because Charles doesn't wanna go, does Shawn not wanna go? I don't get it. I started to go as low as to ask my dad to call him, but I knew I'd feel horrible if I did that. So I'm coming to you, but you're standing there, mum's the word. What? Is there some household loyalty that you're under? Has he told you something he told you not to tell me? Does he not like me anymore? Has he got another girl? What?"

Fed up, Olive blew up. "Okay, Octavia! You're stressin'! I haven't talked to Shawn. Not about you, not about anything. Charles goes in his room, shuts the door, and acts like I don't even exist. Maybe Shawn's pulled away because he knows we are friends, and that's all weird for him, but I'd be speculating at best. I've always known the joker couldn't dance. That could be it. But again, I don't know. So don't ask me to tell you something that I truly don't have the answer for, and don't be all mad at me because I'm not responding. Heck, there his tail is, right over there. Go ask him!"

Shawn looked back, saw the two of them, and then started walking faster. Octavia's insides started bubbling over. Shawn's distant actions were making her queasy.

Octavia said, "Okay, I get the point. I didn't mean to pressure you."

Olive saw Octavia's eyes start to water up and said, "Hey, I'm sorry. I'm not trying to hurt your feelings or anything like that. It's just that I don't want you to think that you're the only one down with boy drama. Sometimes it's like, how can I help you with yours, when I can't even help myself? You know the whole airplane theory? You can't put a mask on a kid if you ain't got the mask on yourself first when oxygen is low."

"I don't got you, but I got you," Octavia said. "Let me catch up to Shawn. Hopefully he has the answers." She ran over to her boo. "Uh, you've been avoiding me, and I don't like it."

"What? You rather me break your heart instead?" Shawn shocked her by saying.

"What is that supposed to mean?" Octavia said, truly irritated with him.

"You've been sweatin' me. I've been getting your messages. Too much pressure. I don't want to go to prom. If I can't live up to what you need, maybe I ain't the guy for you."

Shawn looked at her as if he hated delivering the tough words. She couldn't hold back the tears that fell. This news was devastating.

CHAPTER TEN
Humbling (Pia's Middle)

When Pia arrived in the big city of Atlanta at the World Congress Center, Ballroom A, that held racks of evening gowns that stretched as far as her eyes could see, she was giddy and a little melancholy. Truly, she hadn't thought she would be able to afford to go to the prom. But Willow had kept her word and gotten with Ms. Davis and found out about this charity group, Sisters in Faith, that allowed people to either donate a prom dress and get another one or bring five dollars and purchase a prom gown.

Most of them were pretty much new or gently used. Pia didn't want a handout, but she did want to look amazing. As the tears swelled, Pia was very excited that Ms. Davis cared enough to drive them all to Atlanta and that her girl-friends were there to make sure she had what she needed. That meant the world to her.

"Alright now. We don't have time for tears," Willow said. "It's time to get out and shop on."

"Where do I start?" Pia asked.

"Follow the signs. They are hung from style to color. Start wherever you like. No wrong way to browse," Ms. Davis assured.

"I don't want to shop by myself! We're all up here. Willow? Sanaa? Have y'all gotten your dresses?"

Both of them shook their heads no.

"Octavia? Olive? You guys gotten your dresses?"

"You know I'm not going," Olive said.

"And hot off the press, I'm not going either," Octavia announced.

Pia looked over at Ms. Davis like *Help me, please.*

Ms. Davis nodded and walked over to the girls. "We all came up here with Pia, and while she appreciates how much you all care, she wants to enjoy this time to the max. So, let's all pretend like we've got somewhere special to go. The prom, a wedding, a fun dinner, a cotillion, whatever you want to think of where you could wear one of these beautiful dresses. Humor us. Try on a few. Show us your favorite. I'm trying on one too. You can take selfies and post them up and all have fun."

Pia hated seeing her four friends flare up their noses. "How can I be all excited about prom when my four best friends are looking stank?"

"Uh oh, look at you trying to call us out," Willow said, proud of Pia trying to be hip. "Alright, we'll try on some dresses."

Pia was shocked that having a backbone was all that it took to get the four of them to scatter about. Pia was left with Ms. Davis. The two were pleased that all the girls were going to dream of being princesses.

Ms. Davis said, "It's really sweet of you to share this time. They were all excited to come up here for you, but you want them to find dresses too."

"Why not? Even though Willow's and Sanaa's parents can afford something real expensive, if they find something here, that's great, right?"

"Yes, absolutely."

"But what about Olive and Octavia? I'm really worried about them. I'm actually worried about Sanaa and Willow too. I mean, it's hard to think about being happy when the people you care about are miserable."

"But that's life, Pia. It ebbs and flows."

"I don't understand," Pia said.

Ms. Davis explained, "There're going to be some good times, and there're going to be some bad times. Sometimes you might be up and your friends might be down, but then they might be excited when you're going through bad times. But it's not just about one person. What makes life meaningful is that in your good times, you can spread good cheer to others who are not as happy. You got to be able to lean on each other and be there for each other. There are some things I wish I could change in my own life, you know."

"Like what? You've got it together. Except you never talk to us about your love life."

"Hmm. That might be because you're younger than me. We're not girlfriends."

"But Ms. Davis! Tell me! You don't want me to tell the girls, I won't."

"Well, I'm not going to ask you to keep secrets from them. There's this guy..."

"Ohhhh, so what do you regret? What? He asked you to marry him and you said no?"

"No, it's nothing like that. A niece of mine...but forget it. We'll talk about that later." Ms. Davis hesitated.

Pia was listening, but her eyes locked on a gorgeous gown. "Oh! I like this one!"

"Well, go try it on, girl! That Tiffany blue would look beautiful on you."

Pia picked up the Tiffany blue dress and nine others. The first few dresses Pia tried on were horrible. Too big, or she couldn't zip them, or she didn't like the color or the style. But the first one she'd laid eyes on was the one she saved for last. Before she could slip into it, her cell phone rang, and it was Stephen.

"Hey, beautiful," he said.

"Hey, you."

"What you doing?"

"Trying on dresses for the prom."

"Ah! So you're going to go with me after all?"

"It's not every day a girl gets asked to go to the prom the way you asked me. So yes, I'm working it all out so that I can be your date."

"Lucky me! I'm going to have the most beautiful girl in the place on my arm."

"Stop it. Are you okay?" she asked him.

"You mean about all this stuff with the basketball players and the rape? I'm ostracized, but it's cool."

He continued, "The police have talked to my mom, and I think they're going to make some arrests soon. Those guys might not be able to graduate, or at least they won't be allowed to attend graduation. But don't you worry yourself with all that. Just get a great dress."

Pia hadn't realized that she had the dress fully on because she was looking down as she stepped into it. But when her girls entered the dressing room and started screaming, she looked up and was stunned.

"What's wrong?" Stephen asked.

"Everything's right! I got to go. I'll call you later. I think I found the dress!"

"Oh, you found the dress!" Willow yelled out.

"It's beautiful!" Sanaa said.

"Absolutely perfect on you," Octavia uttered.

"Yeah, girl, you're working that," Olive said.

Ms. Davis just smiled.

When Pia turned around, the five of them had on the dresses they loved too. Everyone had found one. All the girls were smiling. Pia knew all wasn't right in her world, but all wasn't wrong either. Pia knew her friends cared so much for her, and it was humbling.

CHAPTER ELEVEN
Crying (Sanaa's Ending)

The prom was in full swing. Sanaa couldn't believe Willow had talked her into the two of them going. She'd agreed, they'd found dresses and looked beautiful; however, Sanaa had never really wanted to go stag to her senior prom. Somehow, she was doing it anyway.

Sanaa knew Willow wasn't going to just walk into the place quietly. No, she had to put on a show.

"Willow and Sanaa in the house!" Willow sang.

Sanaa truly matched the prom's fairytale theme, looking like Cinderella. She was heavenly in a cotton candy pink dress that was strapless at the top and flared out at the bottom. The rhinestones across the top made it pop.

Though Willow had bought a gown from the dress exchange in Atlanta with the other girls, she ended up wearing a different dress that her mother purchased for her. Willow was working it in this fitted, red-beaded gown. It looked like it cost a thousand dollars.

The two of them were getting looks from a bunch of guys who were without dates. Willow was eating up the attention. Sanaa's eyes searched for a place to sit. As she scanned the room, she froze dead in her tracks when she saw Miles standing at the entrance with Toni. Willow followed Sanaa's eyes and saw what was bothering her friend.

"Oh my gosh! No, his tail didn't walk up in here with that heffa!" Willow hollered.

They watched as Toni and Miles hugged each other real tight. Toni was facing Sanaa. She rolled her eyes hard like, *Gotcha.*

Miles walked away from the dance floor, and Willow said, "Maybe they're not together.

Let's just find a seat and not worry about it. We can have some fun. You didn't wanna come here with him. So if he came with a date, even if it is her, don't sweat it."

The two of them went to find a table, but Sanaa kept eyeing Miles. "See, look. They are together. He brought her punch."

"You need to get a life," Willow told her. "Ain't no use in worrying over spilled milk."

The place filled up so quickly that Sanaa lost track of where Miles and Toni went until later in the evening, when Toni tapped Sanaa on the shoulder.

Toni bragged, "Mighty funny how the guy you thought you'd be coming to the prom with came with me instead."

"Like she cares about any of that," Willow said. "You see us over here worried about you and Miles?"

"Yeah, Sanaa's real worried. Let me go find my boo. Toodaloo!" Toni said, sashaying on.

"Why didn't you let me kick her tail?" Willow said to Sanaa.

When a slow song came on, Sanaa thought

she was going to die. Her heart couldn't stop beating. All she kept thinking about was Miles, out there on the dance floor with his hands all over Toni. While she didn't want his hands all over her, she did wish things hadn't ended so abruptly between the two of them. But she didn't know how to fix it at this point. Willow was right. No need to stress over things that can't be changed. So Sanaa cased the room for a guy to dance with. While she had many suitors looking at her like, *Pick me*, she stayed put, wishing the hour would hurry up and roll on so that she and Willow could roll out.

Suddenly she heard the words, "May I have this dance?" and when her eyes peered up, she was stunned to see Miles, looking good in his black tuxedo, white tie, white vest, and white shirt. She didn't want to get caught up in the moment. She didn't want Toni to see her with Miles.

"No, go be with your date," Sanaa said. She got up to try to walk away, but Miles walked faster and stepped in front of her.

"Hold up. I came by myself. You did too, right? What's wrong with us dancing?"

"What do you mean, you came by yourself? Why you lying to me?" Sanaa questioned.

When she tried to move him out of the way, he stood firm. "I'm not lying to you. Who'd you think I came here with?"

"Toni. Quit playin'. Dang, this is hard enough."

"What, you jealous?"

"Oh, so now you admit you came with her?"

"Oh no, that's not what I'm saying, but you're all up in arms, thinking I came with Toni when that's a lie."

"I saw you two."

Willow rushed over. "Ooh, girl, I gotta tell you, Toni was lying!" Then she saw Miles. "Oh, I guess you already know."

"Nah, she thinks I came with Toni. You might wanna tell your friend the truth."

"Girl, she over there with the girls, looking pitiful, moping like you were doing," Willow said. "She is not here with him."

"Why we see them together?" she said to Willow. Turning to Miles, she said, "You hugged her. You gave her punch. All that stuff."

"I walked in, and she was right there. She gave me a hug, said I looked good. I told her hey. She said she was thirsty. I'm a gentleman. I got her something to drink. I didn't come with her. The rest of the night, I've been searching for you. Can we put all that aside and have this dance? You didn't wanna come with me. The least you can do is be with me now that you see you care about a brotha, right?"

"Right?" Willow said, putting in her two cents.

Sanaa couldn't say hush because her girl was telling the truth. "Okay."

Another slow song came on, and Miles guided Sanaa out to the middle of the dance floor and put his arms respectably around her lower waist. He leaned over, kissed her on the cheek, and said, "You're gorgeous. You look like a princess tonight. I'm sorry for coming on so strong. I'll take you any way I can. Even if that means I gotta keep my hands off you," he said as he put his hands down, teasing.

As she became emotional and the tears started flowing, she lifted his hands up and put them back on her waist. "No. I know you can be respectful. You holding me does feel really good."

He said, "Alright. If I'm making you feel good, then please, no crying."

CHAPTER TWELVE
Caring (Willow's Ending)

"Wow, they look so sweet," Willow uttered to herself as she watched Sanaa and Miles waltz on the dance floor.

"Okay, they do look sweet. But who are you talking to?" Octavia asked, startling Willow.

Willow got up and gave Octavia a very big hug. "Oh my gosh, look at you! I thought you weren't coming."

"My dad talked me into it. Said he regretted not going to his prom. And since I had a dress and all and you guys were set, why should I sit at home and mope? I'm about to go to college. Shawn's loss."

"That's wassup. I like the way you talking."

"Even though I wish he was here...," Octavia said.

"Oh no, no, no. We are not having none of that. This is not the pity party table. Sit. Let's have some us time," Willow said as she put her arm under Octavia's.

"How're your mom and dad doing?" Octavia asked.

"Good. I ain't heard a bunch of arguing. One day I heard screaming, and I thought they were throwing down. But when I got close to the door, I think they were throwing down another way. You know what I'm saying?"

Octavia just giggled.

"What? They're married. They're adults. Certainly them getting busy is a good sign. You approve of that. My momma's a pastor, but she ain't stupid. I'm sure she does what it takes to keep her man."

"You are so fearless," Octavia said. "I've gotta take me some of your fiery spirit with me to college next year."

Willow smiled, truly flattered, and then

said, "So you haven't heard from Shawn at all?"

"I thought we weren't going to mention his name," Octavia teased.

"Well, I know you care about the guy. So I'm just asking you. Has he called to apologize or anything? You can't tell me that he ain't really feeling you."

"I thought he was. I thought we had something good going. He was even connecting with my dad. But he pulled back from hanging out with my father, too, lately. Like I care that he doesn't have money for prom. It's not like I'm rich, ya know?"

"You guys think I am, but I'm not. So yeah, I know."

"Whatever, Miss Gorgeous Red Glittery Gown. That's not the one you picked out when we were in Atlanta."

"Naw, my mom wanted me to splurge. I look good, don't I? Too bad I'm not looking good for anyone."

Willow was surprised she was sharing her inner thoughts with Octavia. She had always been so closed, not really wanting to let anyone in. Sure, she'd had an acquaintance on the dance team, but in reality she was her own best friend until a few months ago. And now, whether it was Sanaa, Olive, or Pia who could have been sitting there instead of Octavia, Willow would have been okay being real. That openness surprised her.

"So you give me a hard time about caring about Shawn, but clearly you wish you weren't alone tonight," Octavia joked.

"I don't know. Maybe I was just too hard on Dawson." Willow thought about the fight that broke up their relationship. She just didn't understand why he wouldn't get physical with her, like all the other guys she'd been with.

"And if Dawson were here right now, what would you say to him?" Octavia asked.

"That I knew he cared about me all these years, living right next door, always there to lend a shoulder when I needed to cry on it. And all he wanted to do was take things slow, and I couldn't handle that."

"So would you ask him for another chance?"

"It's not like he'd give it to me."

"How do you know what he'd do?" Willow heard Dawson say huskily behind her.

Willow looked at Octavia, who motioned for Willow to turn around. "Wow, Dawson . . . you're here."

Dawson said, "Yup. Holding out my hand to take you on a stroll so we can talk."

Willow had to admit, he looked so darn fine in his white jacket, black tie, and black trousers. He cleaned up real well. She was impressed.

"She'd love to go on a walk with you," Octavia said as she pulled Willow up out of her seat.

Dawson escorted Willow to the dance floor. "That dress looks really nice on you."

"I'm not trying to entice anyone or anything," Willow said, knowing they'd had trouble in that area before.

"Look, a brother ain't blind." He stopped walking and made eye contact with her.

Willow felt confused. "I know it's your prom too, so I'm not wanting to ask why you're here, but why are you around me? Why do you want to give me another chance?"

"Because ever since I was in the fifth grade,

and you came to school with those stupid pig-tails and kicked me in the shin and I realized you were my next-door neighbor, I knew that you were the girl for me."

"I'm sorry I've been so mean. I guess I don't know how to be nice to somebody who is true. Can you ever forgive me?"

"Nothing you could do or say..." Dawson said as he touched her brow and kissed her cheek, "would ever make me stop caring."

CHAPTER THIRTEEN
Overwhelming (Olive's Ending)

Olive sat in her room, wanting to hurt somebody, break something, or cry. It was prom night, and she knew Charles was in the house. Even though they weren't at prom, she at least wanted to be watching a movie with him. A scary one, so they could curl all up and enjoy each other. But he'd been distant. She'd hoped that he'd come around and forgive her for meddling, but he hadn't.

She had to get over it. She knew having a pity party wasn't going to fix anything. Living in a foster home, she'd always been tough. But somewhere between ninth grade and twelfth grade, she'd lost a little of that toughness after getting together with Tiger.

Olive got down on her knees and cried out, "Lord, I need you to make things right. I've done all I can. I messed up. I'm not perfect, but I've asked for forgiveness. I believe that you haven't forgotten me. Just help me not break."

Suddenly, she got a text from Ms. Davis that read, "Why are you looking so melancholy?"

She quickly texted back, "Huh!?"

Olive got a reply from Ms. Davis, "Turn around. I'm by your door, and I got something that's gonna make you smile."

Olive turned around and couldn't believe it. Ms. Davis was standing there with the very short and sassy yellow dress that Olive had picked out in Atlanta.

"It's time for you to get ready to go to the ball," Ms. Davis said.

"What am I supposed to do? Go by myself? No, thank you. I know my girls are at the prom, but not me. I don't wanna go by myself."

"If you accept my humble apology, you don't have to go alone," Charles said, appearing from the darkness of the hallway to stand by Ms. Davis in the doorway.

He was decked out in a handsome tux, all white. The look on his face mirrored what his apology said. She could tell he was sincere. As Ms. Davis moved out of the way and Charles entered the room, Olive stood still.

"I would give y'all some privacy, but I promised Ms. B that I would supervise. I don't like the fact that the two of y'all could be left alone in this bedroom, so I'ma stand right here. Pretend like I'm not here," Ms. Davis said as she smiled.

They both smiled back. Olive knew there had been plenty of times her and Charles had been alone in a bedroom, but if it made Ms. Davis feel better playing watchdog, she was fine with it. She just couldn't believe the guy she cared so much for was now doing a 180.

Charles confessed, "Ms. Davis talked to me at school. I never knew having counseling could be so enlightening. I'm angry about the decisions I made and for trying to push you away. But I know that if you wouldn't have stepped in, I wouldn't even be in the position to graduate now. I'm just lucky you went out of your way to convince the judge to let me stay in this house. Ms. Davis and I went to the judge and asked if I could go to prom."

Olive motioned for an answer as her eyes opened wide. Charles pulled up his left pant leg, and she saw the monitor had been removed. She clenched her heart.

"Where is it?" Olive asked.

"Well, it's not gone for good. Ms. Davis will take me back tomorrow morning to put it back on."

Olive went over to the door. "You would do this for us?" she asked Ms. Davis.

Ms. Davis responded, "What can I say? I told you I'm a hopeless romantic. It's a lot I'm trying to make up for. My niece just—"

"Your niece?" Olive asked, confused about what Ms. Davis was alluding to.

Pulling back, Ms. Davis said, "Forget it. You get dressed. We don't have a lot of time left at the prom."

Olive hesitated. Though Charles was handsome and the dress was all that and a bag of diamonds, Olive suddenly felt unworthy. She needed more than a bath to become flawless.

"Do you wanna go to the prom or not?" Ms. Davis messed with her and said. "I'll go with this handsome guy if you don't want to."

Olive winked and said, "Oh, but what about the boyfriend of yours Pia was telling all us about? He probably wouldn't like that."

Ms. Davis laughed. "Exactly. So don't get me in trouble. Get ready to go out with your boo."

Olive leaned in and whispered, "But my hair, my makeup."

"Girl, as natural and pretty as your hair is, don't trip," Ms. Davis said. "Alright, out, Charles."

He said, "Just one second, Ms. Davis, please."

"Okay," Ms. Davis offered.

He grabbed both of Olive's hands and said, "I am so sorry for being a jerk. All you did was care for me, and I made life miserable around here for no reason. I missed you. I've been thinking about you. Hurry up, so I can see you gorgeous. I mean, you're gorgeous right now, but I know you 'bout to be . . ."

Olive took one finger and placed it over Charles's mouth. After he hushed up, she removed her finger. She bent his neck down and gave him a sweet kiss.

It took her and Ms. Davis all of thirty minutes to get her ready to go. Olive looked drop-dead gorgeous when she stepped out in a beautiful, stellar, banana yellow gown. Charles was coughing.

"It doesn't look right?" Olive uttered, feeling self-conscious.

"Are you kidding me? You look beautiful. Do I give it to her now?" he said to Ms. Davis.

"Yes."

Charles took out a sweet box with a yellow rose in it and said, "I see your eyes watering up, looking at this flower like it's the most precious thing."

"I just can't believe we're going to prom. I just can't believe this. You just don't know what this means to me."

"You don't know what it means to me for you to forgive me, because as nice as this flower is, it pales in comparison to how beautiful it's gonna be on you."

At that moment, he pinned the flower on her dress. Then they walked out arm in arm and got in the back of Ms. Davis's car. Olive felt so special, so appreciated, and so loved. All those feelings cupped together were absolutely overwhelming.

CHAPTER FOURTEEN
Loving (Octavia's Ending)

"And the winner of the Jackson High School prom queen is Octavia Streeter!" Ms. Sealy, the Student Government Association advisor, said in a bubbly tone.

Octavia hit herself. She wondered why in the world she was daydreaming so hard. To believe her name was called was stupid. When Willow and Sanaa rushed over, clapping like everybody else, she wondered if she was still sleep.

"Get up, prom queen!" Sanaa said, trying to lift Octavia.

"Represent us! Swoop list in the house! That will show them not to mess with us. Popularity has its perks. Go on, prom queen!" Willow beamed, all proud.

Stunned, Octavia shared, "But I didn't even know my name was on the ballot."

"I put it there," Willow proudly announced. "I figured you'd have the best chance of all the swoop girls. I knew what would happen at a majority black school, just like with homecoming earlier in the year; too many of us cancel each other out. As I thought, you, as the only white girl, would get the most votes. Go get 'em!"

"You put my name on the ballot?" Octavia said, not wanting to move.

"Yeah, why?" Willow said, wondering why Octavia was tripping.

Getting wimpy, Octavia cried out, "I don't deserve y'all's love!"

Willow smacked her lips. "Girl, if you don't get your butt up there . . . no time to be mushy. You know we care."

"Yeah, but like this. I never won anything in my life," Octavia replied, completely flabbergasted.

"And they going to take the crown away from you right now if you don't hurry up and get on up on stage," Sanaa said playfully.

"Do I look okay?" Octavia asked, adjusting her melon-colored, fitted, satin gown.

"Yes, your red locks and curls look fine. Plus you're accenting them hips. Go!" Willow uttered.

Never in her life had she felt so special. Prom queen . . . the feeling was surreal. As Octavia was walking to the podium, she passed Pia and Stephen.

"Congratulations!" Pia said as she blew kisses.

"Where have y'all been?" Octavia asked.

Pia said, "Long story. Dinner was late. But look who we found . . ."

Pia pointed behind her. It was Olive and Charles. Octavia smiled really big, but Olive and Charles both knew she was a little melancholy when she looked around and didn't see Shawn. Staying focused on her moment, Octavia reached the stage and was given the crown.

Ms. Sealy turned back to the mic, and with hype she said, "And the winner of the Jackson High School prom king is Shawn Fox."

Octavia's eyes practically popped out of her head. She knew Shawn wasn't there, but the fact that both of them won was more than ironic.

Ms. Sealy leaned in and said, "Yeah, when all the other nominated boys saw Shawn's name was on the ballot, it was when he in the hospital suffering from the gunshot wounds. They felt sorry for him, so they took their names off."

"He won by default?" Octavia asked.

"No . . . respect," Ms. Sealy boasted as if she was proud of the students' stance on the matter. "Where is he? We called him."

Octavia said, "Sorry, but he's not . . ."

Cutting her off, Ms. Sealy shouted, "Oh, there he is! Shawn, come on up!"

Octavia dared get her hopes up and think Shawn was there, but when she looked up she saw Shawn standing beside a gentleman she knew all too well. He was with her father. Most girls would be all upset if their dad was at their senior prom, but she knew there was more to the story.

As Shawn took his time getting to the front, people clapped, knowing all he'd endured. He made his way to the stage and accepted his crown.

Ms. Sealy said, "Now it's time for our king and queen to dance."

Shawn motioned for her to lead the way. Every part of Octavia was shaking. Though she knew this was reality, it felt more like a dream. One she didn't want to wake up from. Thankfully, this was her reality. But she was still trying to connect the dots. She was still angry at Shawn for giving her grief about the prom in the first place.

"Should I even dance with you?" Octavia said, having mixed feelings about it all. "After the way you treated me."

Shawn took a deep breath and vulnerably shared, "I know. How could I tell you I was ashamed? Ashamed for not having any money to get a tux or rent a limousine, take you to dinner, buy pictures, or even get a corsage, for goodness' sake. So much has happened to me in the last couple months, I can't even believe I'm standing here. Worse than that, though, I can't believe I treated you so mean."

"Did my father help?"

"Yeah, he did. He let me borrow his jazzy suit. Shucks, it looks like a tux," Shawn said as they both smiled.

Octavia moved towards him, and they started dancing. They got a lot of oohs and ahhs. They both enjoyed the moment and danced in silence.

As soon as the dance was over, Octavia rushed up to her father. "You helped him?"

"Yep. I didn't go to my prom because I couldn't afford it. And while he won't be taking you back home in a horse and carriage, he can take you out. Sometimes, in order to feel alright, you've got to give back. Shawn's a good kid. It's not his fault his parents walked away. But when he got word he was going to be prom king and felt terrible he'd let you down, he reached out. I was happy to help make it happen. My black suit looks pretty good on him, huh?"

"Yeah, Dad, it does," she replied with a laugh. Octavia knew she was blessed. "Dad, how can I ever repay you?"

Her father explained, "Just keep doing the right things. Keep caring about people and doing your best. You've got one of the biggest hearts I know. How could I not do all I can to help you when you're so loving?"

CHAPTER FIFTEEN
Shining (Pia's Ending)

Pia felt on top of the world. All finally seemed right, not only for her, but for her four swoop list friends as well. Though she and Stephen were late to the prom, they made it just in time to see Octavia crowned queen. She knew life wasn't always going to be perfect, but she was so thankful for the moment of happiness.

Earlier in the month, she was feeling so guilty about being the only one going to prom, or at least the only one going to their senior prom with a date. Now she was thankful all five of them were with guys they cared about. Who knew things would turn around the way they did? She made a mental note: *Just because you're down one moment and it seems like there's no hope doesn't mean things can't turn around in an instant.*

Her mom had been doing better. Waitressing wasn't bringing in much money, but it was giving her a purpose. In the whole month, she hadn't entertained a male friend. Pia was amazed.

"You want something to drink?" Stephen asked, being really attentive.

"That'd be great," Pia said.

He kissed her on her forehead and walked across the room to the punch bowl. Pia loved his gray, pin-striped tux. As she sat alone, she hoped things would stay great for a very long time.

Her thoughts were interrupted by Ms. Davis. "Hey, beautiful gal, penny for your thoughts?"

"Ms. Davis! Hey, how are you?"

"Look at your friends. A couple of weeks ago, they didn't even want to try on a dress. Even though Miss Willow got a different one, you all are stunning!"

"I know. I was just sitting here thinking the same thing. Thanks to you."

"I was happy to take you all."

"No, I mean thank you for putting this all together and just always being there. It's like you know what we need. You go above and beyond. It means a lot."

"I'm thrilled to see you all in a stronger place. The swoop list could've devastated your lives for good, maybe even ended them," Ms. Davis shared in a caring and concerned tone. "But you all have taken the advice given and overcome your struggles."

When Ms. Davis said that, Pia was intrigued. The five of them had wanted to get to the bottom of all the secret letters they got from the dead girl, Leah, but they hadn't pursued that. Pia wanted to make sure they delved into it.

"Okay, Ms. Davis. I'ma go talk to the girls," Pia said, giving her a big hug.

"Yeah, go talk to them. I'm just proud of you guys, that's all."

Pia walked toward the ladies' room. She knew the other four were in there. They'd asked her to go, but she was sticking around with Stephen. Since he was getting something to drink and she was feeling motivated to find out more about Leah, she went to find them.

She told them, "Look y'all, we gotta stick to the plan and figure out those notes."

"We hear you, Pia," Willow said. "Let's enjoy the night. You knew for weeks you were going with Stephen. All of us are still trippin' that things have worked out. We got you with Leah."

"Yeah," Sanaa said, "we got you with Leah, but we're basking right now!"

"Okay," Pia threw up her hands and said. Her friends were right. She could worry about the Leah mystery some other time.

As the five of them were exiting the bathroom, they stopped dead in their tracks as they were approached by a group of cheerleaders. It wasn't Toni and the girls from the dance team who had already given them so much drama. No, those girls were still over pouting somewhere. But things weren't all good with Pia's cheerleading crew, either. Claire, her best friend on the squad whom she hadn't talked to in months, was beside Chancey, a mean cheerleader who never liked Pia.

"What is it now?" Willow said, stepping in

front of Pia. "You got somethin' to say to her, you can say it to all of us."

"Yeah," Olive said, stepping up too. "I'm really tired of the girls in the school. I'm not tryna fight, but I'm not trying to see y'all come down on my girls either."

"No, you guys misunderstand," Claire said. "We came to thank y'all."

"Chancey came to thank me, Claire? Come on," Pia uttered, actually stepping up for herself.

Chancey said, "We came to thank you guys for talking to our sisters in middle school."

"Yeah, Pia, you don't remember, but Christy had really been out there," Claire shared.

"And my sister Katheryn, she's been quite wild too. You guys had a big influence on a lot of girls over there, and we just came to let you know it made a difference. Sorry I've ever given you grief," Chancey said. "Forgive me."

The girls all shook hands, hugged, and complimented each other on their dresses and attire. Then, all smiles and giggles, the five swoop list girls went out to the dance floor as a fast song came on. Though their dates were looking on, it was girl time. They took to the middle of the floor and enjoyed themselves.

"You know what tonight is?" Willow asked.

"Sure do," Pia uttered as they sashayed to the beat. "Time for a slumber party!"

Sanaa saw Toni and her crew giving them stank looks. "What we gonna do about those haters?"

"Nothing," Olive said. "We can't fix unhappy people. I learned that the hard way. Bad as I wanted to change Charles, things didn't work out until he decided he was wrong."

"I feel you, though, Sanaa," Octavia said. "It's good you want to make everyone feel as great as we do."

"Well, let's discuss the state of Jackson High later. Right now it's groove time," Pia yelled out.

Pia was a great dancer and had no problem leading the way. As her hips swayed back and forth, she realized true happiness wasn't about having everything right. True happiness was about feeling a sense of pride, doing the best you can, and giving more than you take, because then and only then is a person really shining.

ACKNOWLEDGMENTS

Feel real good . . . we all want a sense of peace and happiness in our lives. If you want to lessen your drama, don't just take, but give! Caring for others will fill you in ways that will make you truly whole. Here's a great big thanks to all who help me feel great about my writing career.

To my parents, Dr. Franklin and Shirley Perry, I feel good because of your wonderful example. You showed me how to never give up. To my publisher, especially Emily Harris, I feel good because you all are taking a chance on another series. To my assistants Ashely Cheathum, Alyxandra Pinkston, and Candace Johnson, I feel good turning in my books because of you all. Your input is invaluable. To my dear friends, I feel good because you don't judge me. To my teens, Dustyn, Sydni, and Sheldyn, I feel good seeing you grow into your own. Your development has blessed me and allowed me to bless others with my pen. To my husband, Derrick, I feel good that you're always there. Your constant presence in my life has afforded me the opportunity to live my purpose. To my readers, especially kids in Jackson, GA, I feel good that this series will make a real difference. Your being open and honest in our sharing session helped me bless others—I believe that becuase we tackled this tough subject, we will make a difference. And to my Heavenly Father, I feel good because no matter what goes wrong You are there. Your love for me holds me together and truly makes me whole.

ABOUT THE AUTHOR

STEPHANIE PERRY MOORE is the author of more than sixty young adult titles, including the Sharp Sisters series, the Grovehill Giants series, the Lockwood Lions series, the Payton Skky series, the Laurel Shadrach series, the Perry Skky Jr. series, the Yasmin Peace series, the Faith Thomas Novelzine series, the Carmen Browne series, the Morgan Love series, the Alec London series, and the Beta Gamma Pi series. Mrs. Moore is a motivational speaker who enjoys encouraging young people to achieve every attainable dream. She lives in the greater Atlanta area with her husband, Derrick, and their three children. Visit her website at www.stephanieperrymoore.com.

READ ALL THE BOOKS IN THE
SWOOP LIST SERIES:

STEPHANIE PERRY MOORE

THE SWOOP LIST · SANNA

GIVE IT UP

STEPHANIE PERRY MOORE

THE SWOOP LIST · WILLOW

ON YOUR KNEES

STEPHANIE PERRY MOORE

THE SWOOP LIST · OLIVE

BACK THAT THING

STEPHANIE PERRY MOORE

THE SWOOP LIST · OCTAVIA

FEEL REAL GOOD

STEPHANIE PERRY MOORE

THE SWOOP LIST · PIA

SIT ON TOP

THE **SHARP** SISTERS

Make Something
of It
STEPHANIE PERRY MOORE

Better Than
Picture Perfect
STEPHANIE PERRY MOORE

Turn Up
for Real
STEPHANIE PERRY MOORE

Truth and
Nothing But
STEPHANIE PERRY MOORE

Icing on the Cake
STEPHANIE PERRY MOORE